Karen's Puppet Show

**Other books by
Ann M. Martin**

Leo the Magnificat
Rachel Parker, Kindergarten Show-off
Eleven Kids, One Summer
Ma and Pa Dracula
Yours Turly, Shirley
Ten Kids, No Pets
With You and Without You
Me and Katie (the Pest)
Stage Fright
Inside Out
Bummer Summer

For older readers:

Missing Since Monday
Just a Summer Romance
Slam Book

THE BABY-SITTERS CLUB series
THE BABY-SITTERS CLUB mysteries
THE KIDS IN MS. COLMAN'S CLASS series
BABY-SITTERS LITTLE SISTER series
(see inside book covers for a complete listing)

Little Sister

Karen's Puppet Show
Ann M. Martin

Illustrations by Susan Tang

A
LITTLE APPLE
PAPERBACK

SCHOLASTIC INC.
New York Toronto London Auckland Sydney

No part of this publication may be reproduced in whole or in part, or stored in a retrieval system, or transmitted in any form or by any means, electronic, mechanical, photocopying, recording, or otherwise, without written permission of the publisher. For information regarding permission, write to Scholastic Inc., 555 Broadway, New York, NY 10012.

ISBN 0-590-06586-6

12 11 10 9 8 7 6 5 4 3 2 1   7 8 9/9 0 1 2/0

Printed in the U.S.A.   40

First Scholastic printing, August 1997

*The author gratefully acknowledges
Stephanie Calmenson
for her help
with this book.*

Karen's Puppet Show

Red Light! Green Light!

It was my turn to be It. I love to be It. Especially when we play Red Light! Green Light! The person who is It gets to be the Traffic Light. Being a Traffic Light is a very important job.

I was facing a tree outside the big house. (The big house is only one of my houses. I have two. I will tell you why later.)

"Green light!" I called.

I waited a few seconds. Then I called out, "One, two, three, red light!"

I spun around to see if I could catch any

of my friends moving. They are allowed to move when I am facing the tree. But they have to freeze when I turn around.

"I saw you move, Hannie!" I said.

Hannie Papadakis stomped her foot. She does not like being caught. But I saw her moving fair and square. I had to call her name even though she is one of my best friends. My other best friend is Nancy Dawes. We call ourselves the Three Muske-teers. We like doing everything together. That is because we get along so well. Most of the time, anyway. (Sometimes we fight.)

None of my other friends had moved. Melody and Bill Korman were as still as stones. Melody is seven. Bill is nine.

Maria Kilbourne was frozen in a running position. Maria is eight, by the way.

"Achoo!" Andrew sneezed.

"You moved! Go back to the starting line," I said, giggling.

"No fair," said Andrew. He looked as if he were going to cry.

"I was only kidding," I said. "I know that

was not a real move. It was a sneeze move."

Andrew is my little brother. He is four going on five. He was feeling a little mopey. That is because we had just moved back to the big house. We switch houses at the beginning of each month. Yesterday was the first day of August.

Wait. I have told you about everyone but me. My name is Karen Brewer. I am seven years old. I have blonde hair, blue eyes, and a bunch of freckles. I wear glasses. I wear my blue glasses for reading. I wear my pink glasses the rest of the time.

"Karen! Andrew! Are you ready to come in?" called Daddy. "It is time for lunch."

"I am coming!" called Andrew.

"Me too," I said.

We had been playing all morning and I was hungry. Even traffic lights need a break sometimes.

Saturday Lunch

Saturday lunches at the big house are my favorite. Everything left over from the week comes out of the refrigerator and goes onto the kitchen table. We get to make any weird lunch we want.

I put cold spaghetti with tomato sauce, some tuna salad, and a big pile of potato chips on my plate. Yum.

Little-house lunches are a lot different from big-house lunches. Oh, right. I was going to tell you why I have two houses. I guess this is a good time.

The story starts when I was little. I used to live in the big house with Mommy, Daddy, and Andrew. But Mommy and Daddy were not getting along. They were fighting all the time.

Mommy and Daddy told Andrew and me that they loved us very much. But they did not want to live with each other anymore. So they got a divorce.

After the divorce, Mommy moved to a little house not too far away. She met a very nice man named Seth. Mommy and Seth got married. That is how Seth became my stepfather. Now four people live at the little house. They are Mommy, Seth, Andrew, and me. And there are some pets. They are Rocky, Seth's cat; Midgie, Seth's dog; Emily Junior, my pet rat; and Bob, Andrew's hermit crab.

After the divorce, Daddy stayed at the big house. (It is the house he grew up in.) He met someone nice too. Her name is Elizabeth. She and Daddy got married. That is how Elizabeth became my stepmother.

Elizabeth was married once before and has four children. They are Kristy, who is thirteen and the best stepsister ever; David Michael, who is seven like me; and Sam and Charlie, who are so old they are in high school.

I have another sister named Emily Michelle. (Yes, I named my pet rat after her. That is because I love my sister a lot.) Emily is two and a half and was adopted from a faraway place called Vietnam.

There is one more important person who lives at the big house. She is my stepgrandmother, Nannie. Nannie is Elizabeth's mother. She came to the big house to help take care of Emily. But really she helps take care of everyone.

Do you want to know about the pets at the big house? They are Shannon, David Michael's big Bernese mountain dog puppy; Boo-Boo, Daddy's cranky old tabby cat; Crystal Light the Second, my goldfish; and Goldfishie, Andrew's elephant. (Oops. I mean goldfish.) Emily Junior and Bob live at

7

the big house whenever Andrew and I are there.

When Andrew and I switch, we do not have to take much with us. That is because we have two of so many things. I even have special names for Andrew and me. I call us Andrew Two-Two and Karen Two-Two. (I got the idea for those names from a book my teacher read at school. It is called *Jacob Two-Two Meets the Hooded Fang*.)

Here are some of the things Andrew and I have two of. I have two bicycles, one at each house. Andrew has two tricycles. I have two stuffed cats. Goosie lives at the little house. Moosie lives at the big house. I have two pieces of Tickly, my special blanket. And I have my two best friends. Nancy lives next door to the little house. Hannie's house is across the street from the big house.

So now you know about my two houses and two families. And now I am stuffed because I ate so much! That happens a lot after Saturday lunch at the big house. Ugh. I am going to go to my room to lie down.

Camp Spirit

Ring, ring! I was not able to go to my room just then. That is because the phone rang. I had to answer in case it was someone important. Guess what! It *was* someone important.

It was Claudia Kishi. She is a member of the Baby-sitters Club. That is a business run by Kristy and her friends in Stoneybrook, which is where I live. Kristy is the president.

This summer the Baby-sitters Club was running an arts-and-crafts day camp. It was going to be held at Mary Anne Spier's

9

house. Claudia was in charge. And I was going to be one of the campers. Claudia asked if I was ready to start camp on Monday.

"I am ready," I replied. "Is camp ready for *me*?"

Claudia said she was not sure. She knows I can be a handful. ("Handful" is a word people use to describe me sometimes.) Claudia asked if she could please talk to Kristy.

"Okay. See you Monday," I said.

I called Kristy to the phone. Then I ran to my room. I did not feel like lying down anymore. I was too excited about camp.

I tried on my camp T-shirt. Kristy and her friends had made T-shirts for the campers and counselors. The T-shirts were navy blue with yellow lettering that said STONEYBROOK ARTS CAMP. Each camper got five shirts. I put on matching navy shorts and went downstairs to show off my camp outfit.

"How do I look?" I asked Daddy.

"You look wonderful. But aren't you

10

dressed a little early for camp? It does not start until Monday," he said.

"I am getting into the camp spirit," I replied.

Oomph! Shannon raced in from her walk with David Michael. She jumped up and put her paws on my chest. She almost knocked me down, but Daddy caught me. Shannon gets out of control sometimes because she is a puppy.

"I think Shannon needs a leash inside the house too," I said.

I looked down at my new shirt. It had two big muddy paw prints on it. Boo and bullfrogs.

"Sorry," said David Michael.

I went upstairs and put on my second T-shirt. Then I looked around for Elizabeth and Nannie. They were reading the newspaper in the kitchen.

"How do I look?" I asked them.

"Terrific," replied Elizabeth.

"Now that you are here, how about

putting away these dishes?" said Nannie.

"Sure," I said.

"La-la, dee-dee, la-la!" sang Emily. She was sitting in her high chair. She had a cup of chocolate milk in her hands. The cup was shaped like a big crayon with a straw sticking out of the top.

She was shaking the cup while she sang. "La-la, dee-dee, la — "

Oomph! Emily shook the cup a little too hard. The top flew off. Chocolate milk splashed on everything, including me and my T-shirt. Boo and bullfrogs number two.

I went upstairs to change my shirt again. Two shirts down, three to go. I decided to wait until Monday morning to put on another camp T-shirt. (I have a very messy family.)

While I was changing my clothes, the phone rang again. This time Elizabeth answered.

"It is for you, Karen," she said.

I love getting phone calls. Hannie was calling to invite me to her house. Nancy was already there. (Her mom had just dropped her off.)

"I will be right over," I said.

I put on a clean white T-shirt. Then I took my camp spirit across the street to Hannie's house.

Who Needs You?

When I arrived at Hannie's house, I told my friends about the muddy paw prints and the chocolate milk.

"I was wearing a camp shirt because I am so excited about Monday. Aren't you?" I said.

"Um, Karen, there is something I have to tell you," said Hannie. "My mom got a phone call from my aunt yesterday. She and my uncle invited us to visit them for a couple of weeks. They got a new boat and a new puppy! So, well, I am not going to camp after all."

14

"But you have to! You signed up. Camp will be fun," I said.

"I cannot stay here if my family goes away," replied Hannie.

"Maybe you could stay at my house. I will ask Daddy and Elizabeth. The Three Musketeers should stick together," I said.

"Thanks. But I have to stick together with my family," said Hannie.

"That is too bad. You will be missing out on so much fun. I guess the Two Musketeers will just have to go to camp without you," I said.

"I do not think so," spoke up Nancy. "You see, I am not going either."

"*What?*" I could not believe what I was hearing.

"I said I am not going to camp either."

"Why not? Did your aunt and uncle get a new airplane or something?" I asked.

I knew that was not a nice thing to say. But I was upset.

"I just plain do not want to go. I want to hang around this summer. I do not want

to have plans every day," said Nancy.

"Bor-ing!" I said.

"Maybe for you. But it is what I want to do," said Nancy. "And it will not be boring. Mommy and Daddy said they will take Danny and me special places sometimes." (Danny is Nancy's brother.)

"But Danny is just a baby. Maybe the reason you want to stay home is because you are a baby too," I said.

"That is mean," said Hannie.

"You are being mean. You are being deserters," I replied. "But you know what? I do not care. The One Musketeer will be at art camp — me. And I am going to have a very good time. So who needs you?"

I stormed out of Hannie's house. I was gigundoly mad at my two friends. But I was not going to let that stop me. I was going to camp. I was going to have fun with or without them.

The First Day

On Monday morning when my alarm clock went off, I jumped out of bed in record time. Sunlight was pouring through my window. It was the perfect day to start camp.

"Good morning, Moosie!" I said. "Too bad you do not get to go to camp. No stuffed cats allowed. Hannie and Nancy do not get to go either. No meanie-mo deserters allowed."

I put on a clean camp T-shirt and went downstairs for breakfast. Kristy was wear-

18

ing her camp T-shirt too. She was on her way out the door.

"Ooh, can I go with you?" I asked.

"I am sorry," said Kristy. "Campers come at nine. See you later."

Part of me wanted to go to camp early. The rest of me wanted to stay home and eat breakfast. I was hungry. I ate three of Nannie's blueberry pancakes with butter and syrup. I washed them down with a glass of milk. Then Daddy drove me to Mary Anne's house.

I already knew most of the kids who were going to camp. There were the younger Pike kids: Vanessa, who is nine; Nicky, who is eight; and Margo, who is seven. (Their older sister, Mallory, is in the Baby-sitters Club and was going to be one of the counselors.) There were the Arnold twins, Marilyn and Carolyn, who are eight; and Jamie Newton, who is four. (Kristy asked Andrew to sign up, but he wanted to take swimming lessons instead.) There were also three kids from my school: Natalie Springer and Omar

Harris, who are in my second-grade class; and Ebon, Omar's brother, who is in first grade.

"Hi, Karen!" said Natalie. "I am excited about starting camp, aren't you? Hey, where are Hannie and Nancy?"

"They decided not to come," I said. I said it as if I did not care.

Tweee! Tweee! A loud whistle blew.

"Attention, campers!" called Claudia. "Everyone over here, please."

We gathered around her.

"As you all know, my name is Claudia Kishi and I am your camp director," said Claudia.

She introduced the counselors: Kristy, Mary Anne, Mallory, Jessi Ramsey, and Stacey McGill.

"Stoneybrook Arts Camp is about having fun and making great things," continued Claudia. "Today we will start with an easy project, as a way to get to know each other. Kristy, will you tell everyone about the project?"

"Sure," replied Kristy. "You may make anything that could go in a circus. When you finish, we will put all of your projects together. Any questions?"

"No questions!" I called over my shoulder. I was already on my way to the supplies table. It had been covered up when we came in. But now we could see everything.

I took one look and knew I was going to love this camp. I saw a rainbow of paper, glitter, glue, fat pipe cleaners, skinny pipe cleaners, and lots of other good stuff.

I knew what I wanted to make and got right to work. I took a bunch of pipe cleaners and bent and curled them to make arms, legs, a body, a neck, and a head. I made a paper hat with glitter and a pom-pom on top. I worked very hard. When I finished, I had made a clown.

"Beep, beep! Coming through," called Omar. He had made a cardboard clown car.

We looked at his car. We looked at my clown. There was no way my clown could fit in the car. It was too big.

22

Then Natalie showed us her project. She had made a pony. It was tiny. I got an idea. I put Natalie's pony into Omar's car. I put my clown on top. The three of us started to laugh.

"Kristy! Come look!" I called.

Kristy came over and started laughing too.

"Perfect," she said.

She put the things we made into the center ring of the circus. Our first camp project was a big hit. I was gigundoly proud.

Paper, Scissors, Tape, and Glue

When the circus was finished, we ate lunch, then played games. After that the counselors taught us a cheer:

At Stoneybrook Arts Camp we have fun.
We make great things for everyone.
Our camp's the best and so we'll cheer
As loud as we can so you can hear:
WE'RE STONEYBROOK CAMPERS! WE
    HAVE FUN!
WE MAKE GREAT THINGS FOR
    EVERYONE! YAY!

24

Every day that week was as good as the first. That is because we were always doing something different. Here are some of the things we made: tie-dyed T-shirts, lanyard key chains, candles that smelled good, soap sculptures, fingerprint paintings.

Every day I thought I had found the craft I liked best. Then we would learn something different and I liked that too.

One afternoon when it started to rain, we went inside Mary Anne's barn.

"This afternoon we are going to use only paper, scissors, tape, and glue. You may make whatever you like. We will help," said Stacey.

I decided to make a paper chain. Here is how I did it. I gathered lots of colored paper, a roll of Scotch tape, and a pair of scissors. I cut one strip of paper. I made the strip into a loop and taped it closed. After that I cut another strip and looped it together with the first one. I added another loop. And another. And another. Then Marilyn sat down next to me.

25

"Hi, Karen," she said. "Look, I am making a paper chain too. Mine is really long already."

Marilyn held up her chain. I wished my chain were as long as hers. That gave me an idea.

"Let's put our chains together," I said. "We can make the longest paper chain in town."

"Cool," said Marilyn. "If we work hard, we will make the longest paper chain in the state of Connecticut."

"We will make the longest chain in the country!" I said.

"Or the continent!"

"We will make the longest paper chain in the world!" I said.

I started cutting, looping, and taping as fast as I could. So did Marilyn. Our chain was getting longer and longer.

"That looks like fun," said Carolyn. "May I help?"

At first I had thought it might be more

fun if just two of us made the longest paper chain in the world. Then I thought how much fun the Three Musketeers always had together. But I did not have time to miss my friends. I was too busy.

"It is okay with me if you help," I replied.

"Me too," said Marilyn.

"We are making the longest chain in the world," I said.

We made loop after loop after loop. My fingers started getting stiff. My back started getting achy.

"Attention, campers. The rain has stopped. The sun is shining. It is time to go outside!" said Claudia.

"You have all made terrific projects," said Kristy. "But I want everyone to look at the paper chain Karen, Marilyn, and Carolyn have made. It is the longest paper chain I have ever seen."

We stood up and stretched out our chain. I could not believe how long it was. The campers and counselors started to clap.

I do not know if our paper chain was the longest in the world. But it was the longest at Stoneybrook Arts Camp. And that was good enough for me.

A Special Announcement

"Give me an A!" said Claudia.

"A!" I shouted with the other campers.

"Give me an R!" said Kristy.

"R!" we replied.

"Give me a T!" said Mary Anne.

"T!" we said.

"What do you get?" our counselors said together.

"FUN!" we answered.

This was a new cheer our counselors had taught us. We thought this was gigundoly funny because A-R-T spells "art," not "fun."

(I am a good speller and know how to spell much harder words than that.)

"This morning I have a special announcement to make," said Claudia.

"Yes!" I cried.

Whenever my teacher, Ms. Colman, makes a special announcement at school, it is something excellent. And I usually shout out in class. Then Ms. Colman has to ask me to use my indoor voice.

But I was not at school. I was at camp. And we were not inside. We were outside in Mary Anne's yard.

"Why don't you wait to hear the announcement?" said Claudia. "Maybe you will not like it."

"I am sure it will be something good," I replied.

It was! Claudia told us that we were going to hold an art show on the last day of camp. We would sell tickets. The money would be used to pay for art supplies for the next summer.

"Please think about what you would like to make for the show. You can make any kind of art project you want. It is just a few weeks away," said Claudia.

I did not want to waste any time. I started thinking right away. It did not take me long to come up with a gigundoly good idea. It was not just an ordinary idea, either. It was special. I had to ask a counselor if I could do it.

I told my idea to Kristy. Guess what. She loved it.

This was my idea. I was going to make puppets and put on a puppet show. The show is the part I had to ask Kristy about. I knew most kids would just make things. But I wanted to perform, too. Kristy said that would make me a performance artist. This sounded very cool.

The only thing was, I had no idea what my show would be about. I had to think hard. I went off by myself to sit under a tree. I brought a pad and a pencil with me. While I was thinking, I started doodling. I drew faces for my puppets. I drew eyes. Noses. Mouths. Then I drew hair.

Hmm. My first puppet face looked a lot like Hannie. I smiled. Then I sketched another face. Eyes. Nose. Mouth. Hair. My smile got bigger. That is because my second puppet face looked a lot like Nancy.

I got out my eraser. Then I made the noses a little crooked. I made the mouths a little bigger. I opened the eyes wide and made the hair a little wild. The faces still looked like my friends'. But now they looked very silly.

It took me two seconds to decide what my show would be about. It would be about three friends who are supposed to go to camp together. But two of them are meanie-mos and become deserters.

My show would have plenty of action. It would be funny, too. Maybe it would win an award.

I was thinking about my acceptance speech when Kristy announced it was time for lunch.

The Second Announcement

That night at dinner I heard another special announcement. My whole big-house family was gathered. Except for Kristy. She had a baby-sitting job.

"I would like everyone's attention," said Daddy. "Elizabeth and I are going away this weekend. A friend of Elizabeth's is not feeling well. We want to spend time with her."

"I will be away this weekend too," said Nannie. "I am visiting a friend at the shore."

I wondered what was going on. First my friends were deserters. Now my family. I

33

did not like this one bit. David Michael and Andrew did not look too happy either.

"Who will take care of us?" I asked.

"Yeah, who?" said Andrew.

"You do not have to worry," said Elizabeth. "Kristy, Sam, and Charlie will be in charge. And we have asked the Hsus and the Kilbournes to check in."

It was nice that our neighbors would be checking in. But I was not so sure about having Kristy, Sam, and Charlie in charge for a whole weekend. Well, maybe Kristy, since she baby-sits all the time. But she does not baby-sit for a whole weekend.

"What are you worried about?" asked Charlie. "We will not let anything happen to you."

"There is one thing I should tell you," said Sam. "I have invited some spooky monsters to dinner Saturday night. I hope that is okay."

When Andrew heard the word "monsters," his eyes grew wide. I thought he was going to cry.

"If spooky monsters are coming, I am leaving!" said Andrew.

"I was only joking," said Sam.

"We love you kids," said Elizabeth. "We would never leave you if we thought you were not safe."

I figured that was true. I also figured that nothing I could say would change their plans. So I excused myself and went to my room. I had important camp homework to do.

When I got upstairs, I took out a pad of paper and my favorite pen. It was a purple pen with a fat point. It made the letters look nice and chunky.

I wrote at the top of a clean page, in big letters, KAREN'S PUPPET SHOW. (I would have to think of a better title later.)

First I needed interesting characters for my story. Hmm, what should I name them?

I knew I could not name them Karen, Hannie, and Nancy. I did not want everyone to know who the show was about. I needed other names. Hmm. Susan. Betsy. Linda. No.

Those names did not sound right. Lucy. Rita. Josephine. No. The names still were not right. I thought some more.

Then it hit me. I could name the puppet that looked like me Sharon. That sounded like Karen. And I could name another puppet Hannah. Guess who she would be like. The third puppet could be Francy.

I wrote the names below the title. Now all I needed was a story. That was easy. My show was going to be about one nice and loyal puppet, and two meanie-mo deserter puppets. It would have lots of funny parts. All I had to do was write them. For an excellent writer such as myself, that would be easy.

I held my pen to the paper. I was ready to write my first funny line. I thought and thought. But I could not think of anything to say. Hmm. I guess writing is not always easy — even for an excellent writer like me.

Karen's Puppet Theater

A few days later it was raining hard. But you know what? I did not even mind. All of the campers went inside Mary Anne's barn to work on projects for the art show. It was time for me to make my puppet theater. I decided to make my theater from a cardboard carton.

While we were working, some of the counselors told rainy-day jokes.

"Why did the silly billy cut a hole in the top of his umbrella?" asked Jessi.

None of us knew the answer.

"He wanted to see when it stopped raining!" she said.

We all thought this was a very funny joke.

Then Kristy led us in a rainy-day song. It was a long song about Noah and his ark. My favorite part was when Noah builds an ark-y, ark-y made out of hickory bark-y, bark-y to keep the animals dry.

"If I made an ark-y, ark-y, I would make it spark-ly, spark-ly. Hey, I will make my theater sparkly, sparkly!" I said to Natalie. (Natalie was making a bouquet of cardboard flowers for the show.)

I wanted to put the sparkles on my theater right away, but I had some work to do first. I needed to cut the carton to make it into a stage. Cutting cardboard is hard, so Kristy helped me.

As soon as I finished cutting, I wanted to put the sparkles on. But it still was not time. I had to paint the carton first. I painted it light blue inside and out.

It looked very good. But it still was not ready for the sparkles. My theater needed curtains. I made them out of red crepe paper and hung them from the top with pipe-cleaner curtain rods. It still was not time for the sparkles.

I made a floor out of dark blue contact paper. Finally my theater looked perfect. It needed only one more thing. Sparkles. I put on lots of them.

"Karen, your puppet theater really is beautiful," said Kristy when I finished.

"Thank you," I replied.

Later, when I got home, a package was waiting for me. Nannie said that Nancy's mom had driven her over so she could drop it off. I guess Nancy was trying to be nice to me. Who cares, I thought.

I took the package up to my room. I did not want to open it because I was still mad at Nancy. But I was curious, so I ripped the paper off and opened the box.

Inside was a mug with my name on it.

The card from Nancy said, *"Hi! I hope you are having fun at camp!"*

I am having tons of fun, I thought. Without *you.*

I put the note and the mug under my bed. I did not feel like thinking about Nancy Dawes.

A Great Idea

On Thursday I started making my puppets. They were very cool. They were paper cutouts that looked like you-know-who glued onto tall sticks I found in Mary Anne's yard.

By the time I was finished, Sharon was a very beautiful puppet with long blonde hair — even longer than mine — and pink glasses with sparkles on the frames. Hannah's hair was black. Francy's hair was reddish brown. I gave both of them goofy expressions.

"Ha! That is what you get for being disloyal deserters," I whispered to the Hannah and Francy puppets when no one was looking. At least I thought no one was looking.

"Um, Karen, are you talking to your puppets? I hate to tell you this, but they are not real," said Margo.

"Thank you, I know that," I replied. "I was just practicing for my show. It is going to be excellent, by the way."

(Sometimes Margo and I do not get along very well.)

When I got home from camp, Nannie said there was mail for me. She handed me a postcard. It showed a seagull sitting alone on the beach. The card said, WISH YOU WERE HERE. I turned the card over and saw Hannie's name at the bottom. Boo. It is fun to get mail. But not from ex-friends.

I thought about putting the card away without reading it. But I was curious again. So I read what Hannie had written: *"I am having so much fun. I hope you are having fun at camp too."*

Yes, Hannie Papadakis. I am having fun. Lots of fun. And I will have even more fun when I put on my show. So there.

I ran upstairs and put the postcard under my bed with Nancy's mug.

Then I thought about my show. I had a theater. I had puppets. My characters had names. But I still had not written a play.

I sat on my bed and thought. But I was having trouble concentrating. That was because I heard music coming from Charlie's room. Sometimes he plays his music loudly. Someone was singing about a friend who let her down. "Down, down, you dropped me down to the ground. Ooh! Ow! Ow!"

Hey, that is just like Hannie and Nancy, I thought. They let me down.

All of a sudden I had a great idea. I decided to make my play into a musical! Instead of writing my play on a pad, I would sing it onto a tape.

I was sure I had an old tape player somewhere. I searched my closet until I found it. Then I found a blank tape.

I cleared my throat and started to sing my very own tune: "Hannah and Francy let me down. They dropped me down in the dirt and I feel very hurt. Ooh! Ow! Ow!"

Pizza Express

On Friday camp was so much fun. The day was very hot. So after we worked on our art projects, we played a game of water-balloon dodgeball. It was the campers against the counselors. We all got soaking wet.

Kristy and I were still soggy when we returned home. Daddy, Elizabeth, Nannie, and Emily were waiting to say good-bye. (Nannie had decided it would be easier for the rest of us if Emily Michelle went with her.)

"I hope Kate gets better soon," said Kristy. (Kate is Elizabeth's friend.)

"Thank you, Kristy," replied Elizabeth.

"Have a great time, Nannie. You too, Emily," said Charlie. He gave Nannie and Emily hugs and kisses.

"You have a good time too, kids," said Nannie.

"We will!" said Sam.

"What time on Sunday will you be home?" I asked Daddy.

I hoped he was going to say he would be back first thing in the morning. But he did not.

"We will call and let you know," said Daddy.

He gave me a hug. The next thing I knew Emily and the grown-ups were gone. Kristy, Sam, and Charlie were in charge. Gulp.

"The fun begins!" said Sam. "Who wants pizza for supper?"

"Me," I said. Pizza sounded like a good supper.

"What toppings should we get?" asked Charlie.

"I want plain pizza," said Andrew.

"That is boring," said Sam. "You are getting to be a big boy now. It is time to try new things."

"I do not like new things."

"You can take off any toppings you do not like," said Kristy.

"I will eat pepperoni," I said.

"That is the spirit!" said Sam. "How about you, David Michael?"

"Pepperoni is okay."

"Pepperoni it is," said Sam. "And maybe a few more things for the rest of us."

Sam called Pizza Express.

"We will have one large pizza with everything on it!" he said. Then he turned to me and said, "Do not worry. It will have pepperoni."

Pizza Express says they are always fast. But they are not. Sometimes they take a long time to deliver a pizza. By the time our pizza arrived, I was starving.

Sam opened the box. I took one look.

"Eww! There is no way I am going to eat that!" I said.

On the pizza were mushrooms, pepperoni, peppers, sausage, onions, and some yucky-looking things I did not even know the names of. And it was still not enough for Sam.

"I am going to add hot peppers and pineapple," he said.

"I want to take everything off. But it will still be gross," said David Michael.

"I am hungry!" said Andrew. He started to cry.

"Do not worry," said Kristy. "I will heat up spaghetti for you kids. We have some left over from last night."

Thank goodness. Kristy heated up three bowls of spaghetti. I took mine to the den.

"I do not even want to *see* that pizza," I said.

"I am right behind you," said David Michael.

"Me too," said Andrew.

I could see this was going to be a very strange weekend.

The Drive-in

"Who wants to see a movie?" asked Charlie.

It was almost seven-thirty. David Michael, Andrew, and I were still in the den.

"We *are* watching a movie," I said.

We had turned on a tape of a Tom and Jerry movie. Andrew thought they were the funniest cat and mouse ever.

Boing! Tom, the cat, got hit on the head with a garbage-can lid.

"Come on, kids. You can watch that tape anytime," said Sam. "We want to have fun now that the grown-ups are away. We want to go to the drive-in. And we cannot leave you behind."

I pressed the pause button on the remote control so we could talk.

"What movie is playing?" asked David Michael.

"The movie is called *The Puppet Masters*," said Sam.

"It's about a puppet? I will go!" I said.

Andrew and David Michael were not so excited. But finally they agreed to go too.

We piled into the station wagon. Daddy had left the keys so we would not have to ride in the Junk Bucket. (That is the name of Charlie's rattly old car.)

"Buckle up, everyone," said Charlie.

As soon as we reached the drive-in, Andrew started complaining that he was sleepy.

"I packed some pillows and blankets," said Kristy.

She took them out and made a cozy bed for Andrew in the back of the wagon.

Then she took out the bag of goodies she had packed. I was munching pretzels when the movie started. I watched the movie for a few minutes. All I saw were people.

"When are the puppets going to come on?" I asked.

"There are no puppets, Karen. It is science-fiction week at the drive-in. This movie is about monsters from outer space," said Sam.

"Monsters!" said Andrew, who was still awake. "I want to go home!"

"You do not have to watch the movie," said Kristy. "Just close your eyes and think sleepy thoughts."

"I thought there were going to be puppets in this movie," I said. "If there are no puppets, why is it called *The Puppet Masters*?"

"Because the people act like puppets when the monsters take them over," said Charlie. "I have seen this movie before."

"It sounds awful," I muttered.

"Give it a chance. Maybe you will like it," said Sam.

David Michael and I watched a few more minutes of the movie. David Michael did not like it one bit.

"This is boring," he said.

"Please be quiet anyway so we can watch," said Kristy. "Why don't the two of you play a game? A quiet game."

"I am going to sleep," said David Michael. He curled up in his seat and closed his eyes.

I tried watching the movie. There were no puppets. And I did not know what was going on. Yawn. I tried to stay awake. Maybe the movie would get better. But my eyes kept closing.

I must have fallen asleep for a minute. I shook myself awake.

"What happened? What did I miss?" I asked.

"The space creatures are taking over," said Sam.

That sounded exciting. I tried watching some more. But I felt my eyes closing again. I shook myself awake.

"What did I miss?" I said.

"Karen, are you watching or sleeping?" asked Charlie.

"Watching," I said.

But my eyes closed again. The next time I opened them, the movie was over and the credits were rolling.

Doing Fine

"Who wants a midnight snack?" asked Sam when we got home. "I am going to toast some marshmallows."

I was sleepy. But I love toasted marshmallows.

"I want some," I said.

Sam toasted two marshmallows for each of us. They were gooey and good. My hands and face were all sticky when I finished eating them. Ugh.

"It is time for you kids to wash up and go to bed," said Kristy.

"I am too tired to wash," I said.

"Too tired," said Andrew.

"Me too," said David Michael.

We went upstairs and got into bed, sticky hands and all.

"I guess being a little sticky does not matter," said Kristy as she tucked me in.

The next thing I knew it was morning. I felt stuck to my pillow and did not know why. Then I remembered. Marshmallows. Even my hair and eyelashes were sticky.

"Breakfast!" called Kristy.

"I will be down in a minute," I called. I wanted to wash up.

"Please come right now. We do not want your breakfast to get cold," called Sam.

"Oh, all right," I said.

I went down to the kitchen. Everyone was there.

"Ta-daa! Blueberry pancakes," said Charlie. "Just like Nannie makes."

I looked at the plate of pancakes. They did not look like Nannie's. They were broken into little pieces.

58

"They stuck to the pan," said Kristy. "But they will taste good."

I took a bite of pancake. "This tastes weird," I said. It felt mushy in my mouth. Ugh. I swallowed some milk.

"When is Nannie coming home?" I asked.

"Tomorrow," said Charlie. He took a bite of pancake. "This does taste a little funny."

Kristy looked at the counter.

"Uh-oh. We used baking soda instead of baking powder. Sorry," she said.

"I will make some toast for us," said Sam. "With cream cheese and jelly. I promise I will not ruin it."

The toast was burned. The cream cheese was too thick. There was not enough jelly. But I was hungry. So I ate three slices.

I excused myself to go work on my play. The camp show was less than a week away.

I was halfway up the stairs when the phone rang. I heard Kristy answer it.

"Hi, Mrs. Hsu. Mom said you would call. We are doing fine," said Kristy.

I rolled my eyes. So far we had had really gross pizza, a really boring movie, a really sticky bedtime, pancakes no one could eat, and really burned toast. Fine? I did not think so.

Hide-and-seek

Saturday was rainy, so I spent most of the day in my room. I wanted to work on my musical. I also wanted to hide from my big brothers and sister. But I had to see them at suppertime. That turned out okay, though, because we went to the mall. I ordered a cheese burrito, just the way I like it. And a big lemonade.

By Sunday I had written one very good song for my play. It was going to be the opening song, when Sharon, Hannah, and Francy agree to go to camp together.

I am going to arts camp, the smart camp.
It is what I want to do!
I am going to arts camp, the smart camp.
I am going to camp with you!

I was singing the song into my tape recorder when the phone rang. I heard Charlie answer it. I thought it was going to be the Kilbournes checking in. It turned out to be Elizabeth.

"That is great, Mom. We will see you soon," said Charlie.

Hooray! Daddy and Elizabeth were coming home!

"Who wants waffles?" called Sam from the kitchen.

"They taste good. We did not ruin them," said Kristy.

I went to the kitchen and tried the waffles. Kristy was right. The waffles were not ruined. But they still were not as good as the ones Nannie makes.

When I finished eating, I could not decide

what to do. I was tired of writing. I wished Hannie were home and I were not mad at her. She could have come over. Nancy too. They would think it was cool that the grown-ups were away. I would have fun with them. Boo and bullfrogs. I was getting mad at them all over again for being meanie-mo deserters.

Then I thought of something. I thought I should be having fun even without Hannie and Nancy. I should be having fun with David Michael and Andrew. The grown-ups were gone for a whole weekend and we were blowing it. We were acting like boring babies. I had to do something fast.

"*Psst!* David Michael. *Psst!* Andrew," I whispered. "Meet me in the den."

The three of us slipped out of the kitchen while Kristy, Sam, and Charlie were cleaning up.

"We are missing our chance to have fun," I said. "We need to do something we are not allowed to do before the grown-ups get home."

"You are right," said David Michael. "We need a plan."

We put our heads together and decided to play a game of hide-and-seek with Kristy, Sam, and Charlie. We wrote a note and taped it outside the kitchen door. It said, *"We are in the house, so do not worry. Just try to find us in a hurry."* (Guess who wrote the poem.)

We hid outside the kitchen, then watched the big kids find the note.

"All right, guys, where are you?" called Sam.

"Come out, come out, wherever you are!" said Kristy.

"We better split up. It will be easier to find them," said Charlie.

As soon as they were gone, we slipped into the kitchen. We listened to Kristy and Sam and Charlie call our names while we giggled and ate chocolate-chip cookies. We are allowed only three cookies each when the grown-ups are around. But they were

not back yet. So we ate as many cookies as we wanted.

We were halfway through a giant bag when we heard a car pull into the driveway.

"What do we do now? We lost the kids!" said Kristy.

She sounded worried. We did not want our sister and brothers to get into trouble. So we burst out of the kitchen.

"We are here!" we said.

"Thank goodness!" said Kristy.

Just then the door opened. With big smiles and plenty of crumbs on our faces, we ran to greet Daddy and Elizabeth.

Greetings

On Monday the big house was back to normal. Well, as normal as it ever gets. Nannie and Emily Michelle had had a great time at the shore. And Elizabeth's friend Kate was feeling better.

Someone else was back from a trip too. On my way to camp I saw Hannie.

"Hi, Karen!" she called from across the street.

"Hi," I said back. I did not run across the street to see her.

"Did you get my postcard?" called Hannie.

"Yes. Thank you," I said. "I have to go now. I am in the middle of a very important project at arts camp."

I heard Hannie call good-bye after me. But I made believe I did not hear. And I did not look at her as Charlie drove down the street.

When I got to camp, I put a few finishing touches on my Hannah puppet. I made her look even sillier than before.

Then I wrote a funny new song for my play. It went like this:

> Eenie, meanie, miney, mo.
> Two deserters say, "I won't go!"
> Are they friends?
> I don't think so.
> Eenie, meanie, miney, mo.

I needed to write just two more songs for my play. The rest of it was already written. I had made Hannah and Francy into two really silly meanie-mo puppets. I was doing a good job of getting back at my ex-friends.

That afternoon when I returned home, I saw Hannie and Nancy in Hannie's yard.

"Hi, Karen," called Nancy.

"Hi," I called back. I still would not cross the street.

"Did you get the present I left for you?" asked Nancy.

"Yes. Thank you. I have to go now to work on a camp project. It was so much fun, I took it home with me."

I hoped they felt bad about the good time they were missing. I felt bad seeing them together when I was by myself.

But wait. I did not have to be by myself. There were lots of other friends for me to call. I ran to the phone. I called Melody.

"Do you want to come over and play?" I asked.

"I cannot come today. But thank you for asking," said Melody.

"Sure," I replied.

I hung up the phone. I thought about calling some other kids. But I decided to work on my play instead. It was getting grumpier and sillier by the minute. That was just the way I wanted it to be.

Tickets for Sale

Tuesday was extra fun at camp. Here is why. We made special costumes that we would wear when we sold tickets for the art show. Claudia said we could use any materials we wanted.

"The more attention your costumes get, the better. We want to sell as many tickets as we can," she said.

If anyone is good at getting attention, it is me. I had learned to do a lot of new things at arts camp. I was going to use a few of the things I had learned to make my costume.

I had learned to make a paper helmet. I

made one out of shiny green paper. To make sure it got plenty of attention, I glued two tinfoil antennae to the top. I colored my cheeks green so I looked like a creature from outer space.

I had also practiced writing fancy letters. I made a big cardboard sign to hang around my neck. I put lots of sparkles on it. Then I wrote in my new fancy handwriting:

ATTENTION EARTHLINGS!
COME TO THE
STONEYBROOK ARTS CAMP ART SHOW
TICKETS: $1

When I finished, I modeled my costume for Kristy.

"How do I look?" I asked.

"You look great!" replied Kristy. "I would definitely buy a ticket from you. In fact, I will. One ticket to the Stoneybrook Arts Camp Art Show, please."

"Really?" I said, smiling. "But you do not have to buy a ticket to the show. You can go

72

STONEYBROOK

ATTENTION EARTHLINGS!
Come to the
Stoneybrook ArtsCamp Art Show

Tickets $ 1

for free because you are a counselor."

"That is okay. It only costs a dollar. And it is for a good cause," said Kristy.

She handed me a dollar. I had sold my first ticket. Yippee!

When everyone was ready, we split up into groups and went door-to-door in Mary Anne's neighborhood.

I sold four more tickets.

"Try to sell as many tickets as you can by Friday," said Claudia. "This is going to be a great show and we want lots of people to see it."

At home that afternoon, I went door-to-door selling tickets. (Sam went with me since I am not allowed to do that alone.) But there was one door I would not knock on. That was Hannie's.

Later, I sold tickets on the phone. But there was one number I would not call. Nancy's.

By bedtime I had sold five tickets in my neighborhood, eight more tickets to people

74

in my big-house family, and two tickets to Mommy and Seth.

That made twenty in one day. Pretty good for a green-cheeked creature from outer space.

Shannon, How Could You?

It was Thursday afternoon, the day before the show. I carefully wrapped up my puppets and took them home for a dress rehearsal.

After dinner I lined up Sharon, Hannah, and Francy in a row on my bed. Sharon was wearing a snow-white dress with pink buttons down the front. A big smile was on her face. Hannah and Francy were dressed in purple and green. They were frowning. My puppets were perfect.

"Please do not pinch me," I said in my sweetest Sharon voice.

"Too bad," I said in my mean Hannah voice.

"Take that!" I said in my mean Francy voice. The Francy puppet knocked the Sharon puppet on the head.

I rehearsed the entire play before I went to bed.

When I opened my eyes the next morning, I was very excited! I put on a clean camp T-shirt. I put a white barrette in my hair. (I made sure not to wear purple or green.) Then I went downstairs for breakfast.

"Karen, you can come early with me today to set up if you want," said Kristy.

"All right!" I replied.

I gobbled my breakfast. Then I ran upstairs to pack up my puppets.

"No, no, Shannon, stop! Bad dog! How could you?" I shouted when I got to my room.

Then I burst into tears. David Michael came running. The rest of my family was right behind him. Shannon had already run out of my room.

"What is wrong?" asked David Michael.

I held up what was left of my Sharon puppet. Shannon had chewed the puppet stick into pieces. Sharon's white dress was a torn, soggy mess. And her head was bent.

"I am sorry," said David Michael. "Shannon likes to chew sticks. She did not know it was a puppet."

"She is your puppy. You are supposed to watch her," I said, even though I knew it was not really David Michael's fault.

"Do not worry," said Kristy. "You have time to fix your puppet. Do you have everything you need here at home?"

"Yes," I said.

"Then you stay here. I will set up the puppet theater at camp. You can start your show as soon as you get there," said Kristy.

"I will help you," said Elizabeth to me.

"I will make sure Shannon stays outside.

And I will bring you a new stick," added David Michael.

Everyone was being very nice. I stopped crying and looked for the things I needed to fix my puppet.

Surprise Guests

Making the puppet the second time around was easy. When I finished, Elizabeth drove me to Mary Anne's.

It was a beautiful day, so the show was set up outside on the lawn.

"Look how many people are here!" I said to Elizabeth.

"It looks like the show is a big success," she replied.

I knew it would be an even bigger success once I put on my play.

"See you later," I said.

I saw Kristy. She was waving me over to the barn. That is where I was going to put on my show. The puppet theater was all set up.

"Just let me know when you are ready," said Kristy. "Then I will tell everyone to come inside."

I was so excited, I could hardly stand it. I was rehearsing a few scenes when I saw Mommy and Seth.

"Hi, honey," said Mommy. "Kristy told us you were here. We came to see your puppets."

"You will have to wait a little bit longer," I said. "I want my play to be a surprise."

"We will be sure to get front-row seats," said Seth.

I kissed them good-bye. Then I practiced a little more. Finally I told Kristy I was ready.

"Attention, everyone! It is show time in the barn!" called Kristy.

This was so cool. I got my own special announcement.

Slowly people filed into the barn. Kristy and her friends had set up lots of chairs. Soon they were all filled. We had a full house.

I peeked out into the audience so I could wave to everyone.

Daddy, Elizabeth, David Michael, and Andrew were sitting in one row. Behind them were Sam, Charlie, Nannie, and Emily. I smiled and waved.

Mommy and Seth had found front-row seats just like they said they would. I waved to them too.

I saw my fellow campers and the counselors sitting together on one side. We waved to each other.

I was looking around to see who else had come. That is when I saw them. In the center of the audience were Hannie and Nancy. Oh, no!

The Show Must Go On

I slipped out of sight behind my puppet theater. I could not put on my show. I could not let Hannie and Nancy see it. They would know it was about them. They would never speak to me again!

"*Psst!* Kristy! Kristy!" I called.

"What is it, Karen? I am about to introduce you," said Kristy.

"I cannot put on my show. Hannie and Nancy are in the audience."

"I know Hannie and Nancy are there. I sold Hannie the tickets the other day," said

Kristy. "I thought you would be happy to have your friends at the show."

"But they are my *ex*-friends," I replied. "They will be very upset if they see my show."

"They said they were looking forward to it. They want to see what you have been doing at camp," said Kristy.

Yipes. All this time they had been trying to be nice to me. Hannie had sent the postcard. Nancy had given me the mug. And now they were coming to see my show.

"Karen, everyone is waiting," said Kristy. "You cannot back out now. The show must go on."

I took a deep breath. Kristy was right. I had to put on the show no matter what. Maybe somehow Hannie and Nancy would understand.

"I am ready," I said.

"Thank goodness. I will introduce you now," said Kristy. She stepped in front of the audience.

"Presenting Karen Brewer's original play

84

with music and homemade puppets," said Kristy.

"Here we go," I said to my puppets.

I held up a card with the title of my play, *The Meanie-mo Show*. Then I brought out my Sharon puppet.

"Welcome, everyone. I am Sharon," I said in my sweet Sharon voice.

I brought out my Hannah and Francy puppets next.

"Do not forget to introduce me. I am Hannah," I said in my mean Hannah voice.

"And I am Francy!" I said in my mean Francy voice.

A few people in the audience started giggling. That was a good sign.

"It is almost summer," said Francy.

"I hear there is a good arts camp in town," said Sharon.

"We can all go together!" said Hannah.

The three puppets danced together in a circle while they sang "Arts Camp is the smart camp." After, they sang "I am going to camp with you!" I made them take a bow.

85

Everyone clapped for the wonderful song-and-dance routine.

Then I took my puppets off the stage and held up a sign that said, TWO WEEKS LATER. HANNAH'S HOUSE.

"Guess what. I am not going to arts camp. You have to go without me," I said in my Hannah voice.

"I am not going either," I said in my Francy voice. "You will have to go by yourself, Sharon."

"Boo-hoo-hoo," I cried in my Sharon voice.

"Ha-ha-ha!" laughed Hannah and Francy meanly.

Then Hannah and Francy sang the meanie-mo theme song:

I am Hannah. I am Francy.
We are plain old meanie-mos.
Just ask Sharon. Sharon knows!
Summer camp? Not for Hannah.
Hannah's going to Montana.
Summer camp? Not for Francy.

Summer camp is much too fancy.
We are plain old meanie-mos.
Just ask Sharon. Sharon knows!

By the time I finished singing, the audience was laughing and clapping along. I peeked out to watch.

I could not believe my eyes. Hannah and Francy — I mean, Hannie and Nancy — were laughing and clapping too.

The Three Musketeers

As soon as the show was over, I ran out to find Hannie and Nancy. But I kept getting stopped by my fans.

I got big hugs from Mommy and Daddy and the rest of my family.

"It was a great show!" said Kristy. "Everyone loved it."

"You did a super job. And your Sharon puppet looked perfect," said Elizabeth.

Everyone kept crowding around to congratulate me. My show was a big hit.

I finally found my friends waiting for me

outside. Even though they were smiling, I was still a little scared to talk to them.

"Hi. I hope you are not mad at me," I said.

"At first I was a little mad," said Nancy. "But the play was so funny. And those puppets were not *really* like us."

"We know we are not that mean," said Hannie. "Anyway, I knew the characters were make-believe, because I did not go to Montana."

"You made Hannah and Francy so funny," said Nancy. "But I would have made Sharon a little different. I would have made her a meanie-mo too."

Nancy changed to a meanie-mo voice and said, "What do you mean, you are not going to camp? I, Sharon, say you *must* go to camp! Or else!"

Nancy started giggling.

"No, wait! I would have made Sharon a whiny puppet," said Hannie. She changed to a wimpy, whiny voice and said, "Poor, poor me. You will not go to camp? What will I ever do?"

90

My friends were making fun of me the way I had made fun of them. But they sounded funny. Now I knew why they had laughed instead of gotten mad.

"Who wants to walk around the art show with me?" I said. "I have not seen it yet."

Hannie, Nancy, and I walked around the show together. I had not seen all of my campmates' finished art projects because I had been so busy with my own.

While we walked around, we found food to eat and friends to talk to.

"It looks like camp was fun," said Hannie. "I am happy for you."

"I am happy you both had fun too," I said.

We told one another a little about our summers. We had a lot of catching up to do. We also had plans to make.

Summer was ending. Soon we would go back to school. None of us could change our minds about that. The Three Musketeers would go together.

L. GODWIN

About the Author

ANN M. MARTIN lives in New York City and loves animals, especially cats. She has two cats of her own, Gussie and Woody.

Other books by Ann M. Martin that you might enjoy are *Stage Fright; Me and Katie (the Pest)*; and the books in *The Baby-sitters Club* series.

Ann likes ice cream and *I Love Lucy*. And she has her own little sister, whose name is Jane.

Little Sister

Don't miss # 89

KAREN'S UNICORN

I clapped as hard as I could. One spotlight shone at the back of the tent. Sparkly glitter swirled down from the ceiling like magical snow.

I gasped. "The unicorn!"

A beautiful, pure-white unicorn stepped slowly into the spotlight. Right on its forehead was a long, straight horn with a bit of a spiral, like soft-serve ice cream. Its white mane and tail looked soft and silky. It wore a fancy jeweled bridle on its head and a shiny sequined blanket, but no reins or saddle. The sparkly glitter shone all around it, and the spotlight gleamed. The unicorn looked like it was made out of a magical moonbeam. It was the most gigundoly beautiful thing I had ever seen.

LITTLE APPLE™

BABY-SITTERS™
Little Sister

by Ann M. Martin,
author of The Baby-sitters Club ®

More Titles... ➡

Available wherever you buy books, or use this order form.

Scholastic Inc., P.O. Box 7502, 2931 E. McCarty Street, Jefferson City, MO 65102

Please send me the books I have checked above. I am enclosing $ _____
(please add $2.00 to cover shipping and handling). Send check or money order – no cash or C.O.Ds please.

Name _____ Birthdate _____

Address _____

City _____ State/Zip _____

Please allow four to six weeks for delivery. Offer good in U.S.A. only. Sorry, mail orders are not available to residents to Canada. Prices subject to change.   BLS1096

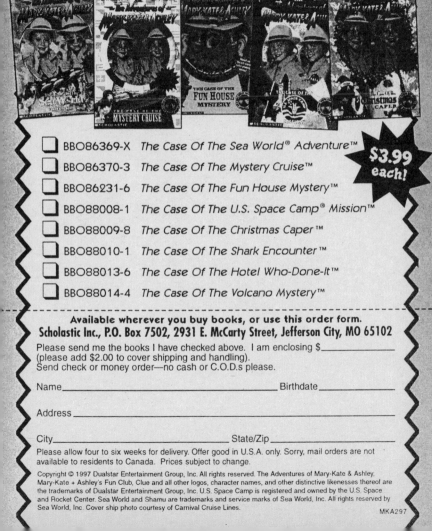